GULAK
THE GULPER EEL

BY ADAM BLADE

ORCHARD

SIBORG'S HIVE LOG

DESTINATION: AQUORA

A plague is coming to Aquora!

Max and that pathetic Merryn girl think they have defeated me, but I have only become stronger. I have analysed Max's weakness — his love for his family! And soon I will take from him all that he holds dear.

I will do something my weak father, the so-called Professor, never could. Take over Aquora! And I won't even need to fire a single shot. The city will be mine, and everyone in it my slaves!

Max couldn't have dreamt up the horror I have in store for him, even in his worst nightmares...

CHAPTER ONE

THE GULPER EEL!

Water shimmered above crusted volcanic vents in the seabed. The temperature gauge on the aquafly's control panel was broken, but Max knew that the sea around the vents was almost hot enough to boil him and his uncle, the Professor, alive. He steered the aquafly towards cooler water, with his dogbot Rivet paddling behind.

After the battle with Kull, the Professor's trilobite Robobeast, Max had repaired the aquafly as best he could. It had been difficult even with the Professor's help and access to his secret lab. The craft's engines and weapons worked now, but some of the sensors had been beyond repair. Luckily, the sonar scanners were still operational.

Rivet dived at the dark purple crabs on the seabed. The dogbot sniffed at them and they snapped at his nose with their bright red pincers. He backed away and barked.

"Leave them alone, Rivet," Max said. The last thing he needed was to offend his friend Lia's father by not looking after the local sea life. He glanced back at the Merryn hunting party following the aquafly. King Salinus rode ahead of his warriors on their swordfish. Glowing ribbons of seaweed trailed from their spears. The hunters had fought alongside Max against a squad of Siborg's cyrates. Now, Max and the Merryn were taking the battle

against Siborg to Aquora.

Lia surged closer on her swordfish, Spike, twirling her spear in one hand. Max met her eye, and she nodded grimly at him.

"This is the edge of the Sea of Fire," the Professor said. "Make sure you keep an eye out for any tricks from Siborg. This would be an excellent place to ambush us."

Cactus-like seaweed dotted the wide stretch

of smooth sandstone ahead, but there was nowhere for an enemy to hide. *Perhaps the pressure's finally getting to the Professor*, Max thought. Max skimmed the aquafly across the desert-like sea floor into the deeper, darker water of the ocean. Neon yellow squid and glowing jellyfish flashed past.

"Max," Rivet barked. "Smell home!"

The screen flickered and a mass appeared on the map ahead. Max would have recognised the shape of the city of Aquora anywhere.

Still, it wasn't going to feel like home when he returned. His cousin Siborg's mindbug infections had made slaves of everyone, including Max's dad. Only humans with the Merryn Touch like Max, his mum and the Professor were safe. Max glanced at the ray-gun the Professor gripped in his hands. *It's our only hope...* If they didn't stop the mindbug infections soon, the people of Aquora would be permanently under Siborg's control.

"Lia," Max called over the communicator. "Remember, your father and his party must be careful now that Siborg's mindbugs can infect the Merryn."

Lia and Spike swam alongside the aquafly. "But we've got a cure now, Max," she said.

The Professor snorted. "The ray-gun can only cure one person at a time, and it needs to recharge between blasts. We have enough to do without having to save Merryn as well."

"There has to be a better way to stop Siborg than using the ray-gun one person at a time," Max said. *We need to cure everyone at once...*

Aquora loomed in the ocean ahead, a twinkling tower of lights. It stretched from the seafloor to the surface, where sunlight glinted off steel structures above the water.

"This is going to be easier than I thought," the Professor said. "Siborg hasn't even sent anyone out to intercept us! My son thinks he's so clever, but I'm smarter."

"I'm not so sure," Max said. His skin was prickling with nerves. "He's always been one step ahead of us before."

"Not this time," the Professor replied. "He knows he's been beaten. My anti-mindbug technology has outwitted him!"

Max kept his mouth shut. Siborg wouldn't let his guard down unless he had a plan.

Suddenly, Aquora's lights vanished. Max gasped as the ocean ahead plunged into darkness. "You see," the Professor said. "Siborg can't even keep the power on!"

"What's that?" Max said. He pointed at the sonar screens. A long tapering shape peeled away from the city. Then a blinking red light like a submarine's distress signal appeared ahead of them.

Max flicked on the aquafly's headlights.

The beams caught a long arrow-shaped head behind the red light. Two tiny eyes, set close together above the narrow slit of a mouth, reflected the headlight back. The creature's lips cracked open then yawned, revealing a chasm-like mouth that was as big as its head. Max took a sharp breath. *A Robobeast!*

It wriggled forward, the overlapping metal plates of its body shimmering like fish-scales. A spiked fin ran the length of its back, dotted with strange lumps. The red light was attached to the creature's whip-like metallic tail. It jiggled the light in front of its open jaws like a fishing lure.

"Let's get out of here," the Professor muttered. "There isn't time to fight Siborg's Robobeasts."

Thrusters burst into life along the snake-like creature's back and the Robobeast surged forward. Max's stomach lurched as he saw King Salinus ride forward on his swordfish,

leading a charge of Merryn warriors.

"No!" Max shouted over the communicator. "Lia, tell your father he's got to keep the Merryn back. We've got experience fighting Siborg's Robobeasts. We can handle it!"

Lia shot towards her father on Spike, but King Salinus waved her away. Two members of the hunting party escorted Lia and Spike back to the Aquafly. "It's no good, Max," Lia said. "He says a king must do his duty!"

King Salinus signalled to his warriors. The Merryn at the front dipped their spears like lances and others raised theirs ready to throw.

"But if we don't do something they'll be fish food," Max said.

"If you really must try to save them, I suggest you use the acid torpedoes," the Professor said.

Max flipped the torpedo switch. Green crosshairs appeared on the interior of the plexiglass watershield. Max grabbed the weapons joystick. He manoeuvred the crosshairs towards the Robobeast and fired. The aquafly rocked as all six torpedoes blasted away, leaving a trail of bubbles.

The weapons exploded in a thick spray of green acid that splattered the creature's head. "Ha!" the Professor yelled.

But the Robobeast kept jetting forward, and the acid slid from its metallic scales. "It's resistant to the acid!" Max said.

The aquafly's speakers hissed into life. "Behold my latest creation," Siborg's mechanical voice boomed. "Gulak the Gulper Eel! It's got a surprise just for you."

Something poured out of Gulak's throat – a buzzing cloud, black as an oil slick.

"Mindbugs, Max!" Rivet barked. Max's heart sank. *He's right!* The tiny black creatures with blinking red lights spread out rapidly through the water towards the Merryn.

Lia was shouting at her father, but it was too late. The swarm engulfed the Merryn warriors before they could turn away.

"No!" Lia gasped. She pressed a pale hand against the watershield. "Father!"

At last the Merryn stopped struggling. King Salinus straightened up on top of his swordfish and nodded to his warriors. "Perhaps it hasn't worked this time?" Lia whispered hopefully over the communicator.

Max shook his head in horror, as the hunting party turned to face the aquafly.

"I don't think so, Lia," he muttered. "I'm afraid they're under Siborg's control now."

Every spear and swordfish pointed at Max and his companions. *We can't fight them without hurting them*, Max thought.

Slowly but surely, the Merryn hunting party began to swim towards them.

CHAPTER TWO

CRASH LANDINGS

Max snatched the ray-gun from the Professor and reached for the aquafly's emergency dome release button. He had to help the Merryn.

The Professor grabbed his arm. "Don't be a fool," he snapped. "You can't save them. The Robobeast will overwhelm us before you've done any good."

"Don't listen to him! We have to save my father!" Lia said over the speakers.

Max looked at her and shook his head. He hated to admit it, but the Professor was right. "We're outnumbered, Lia. We can't beat Siborg if we stay and fight."

Gulak's thrusters fired and the gulper eel swept through the Merryn formation. It knocked hunters from their swordfish while the rest fought to keep control of their mounts. More mindbugs poured from Gulak's mouth, swarming towards the aquafly.

"Lia, quick, inside," Max said. He slammed the emergency watershield release button. Air bubbled out of the compartment as the dome slid open and water flooded in.

Lia bit her lip as she glanced towards her father, who was struggling to keep up with the gulper eel. "It's too late," Max urged. "If you get caught by the mindbugs you'll be infected again. We have to save ourselves before we can save your father!"

At last Lia scrambled off Spike. She had her Amphibio mask ready as she slipped inside the aquafly. The watershield closed and the water drained away.

Mindbugs swarmed around the aquafly. Their metal feet clawed at the watershield. Tiny drill-like probes emerged from their bellies, whining against the plexiglass as they tried to break into the cabin. Spike's tail

thudded against the watershield as he used it to knock the robotic creatures off.

The gulper eel stretched out its huge jaws and slid closer. *It wants to swallow us whole!*

"Get Spike out of here," Max said. "We need to run!"

Lia nodded. Her nose wrinkled as she concentrated on her Aqua Powers, sending a message to her pet. Spike nodded with his sword then dived away into the gloom.

Max stomped on the accelerator pedal. The aquafly charged towards the Robobeast and the remaining Merryn. He gripped the controls tightly to keep the craft steady as the gap between them rapidly narrowed.

Now, Max thought and pulled back hard on the controls. The aquafly tore past Gulak's wide mouth and up over the Merryn spears. The gulper eel whipped round and blasted after them like a rocket.

Max jerked the steering column, heading for Aquora. They'd only be safe from the Robobeast once they reached dry land. Rivet's propellers were struggling to keep up as Gulak's gaping jaws inched closer and closer.

"Rivet, magnetise!" Max told his dogbot over the communicator.

Rivet's paws landed on the aquafly's wing with a clunk. Max rerouted what power he could to the aquafly's engines, but Gulak was catching up fast.

"Has your brain gone soft?" the Professor shouted, glancing anxiously over his shoulder. "Fire your sea-to-air jump-thruster!"

Of course! Max didn't need to reach the city underwater – he could fly to it. He slammed down the jump-controls. The thrusters punched the aquafly upward, jamming Max, Lia and the Professor back against their seats. The craft shook violently as it burst from the water and rocketed into the air.

The glistening steel and glass buildings of Aquora rose up ahead. Enormous banners hung from the tallest high-rises, bearing the grinning half-robotic face of Siborg. Aquora's flags had been replaced with large red eyes on a white background.

He's turning Aquora into Siborgia!

The next moment the engines spluttered and the aquafly plunged towards the city. The control screens flickered, showing that the power levels were exhausted. Max tried to glide the craft towards one of the long highways that snaked through the city, but its wings weren't designed for the job. It was falling faster and faster...

"Brace yourselves!" Max yelled to the Professor and Lia.

CLANG!

The aquafly clipped the edge of a building, and the shock spun them towards the docks. Max tightened his straps and closed his eyes.

The aquafly crashed into the docks and bounced across a loading bay. With each impact the harnesses snapped at Max's chest and stomach. Sparks and screeches erupted underneath the hull as the craft skidded across the steel-plated deck.

"Watch out!" Lia screamed, and Max opened his eyes to see her pointing at the glass-fronted building they were about to hit.

But there was nothing he could do about it. The aquafly had lost its manoeuvring thrusters and wings. "Hold on!" he cried.

Shattered glass rained down on the watershield as they careered into the building.

The aquafly spun inside and slammed into a pillar. Max was thrown back against the control seat. Smoke filled the cabin, stinging Max's eyes and making him cough. Fires burned across the smashed entranceway.

Max checked on the Professor and Lia. They were dazed, but they didn't look seriously hurt. He slammed the watershield release

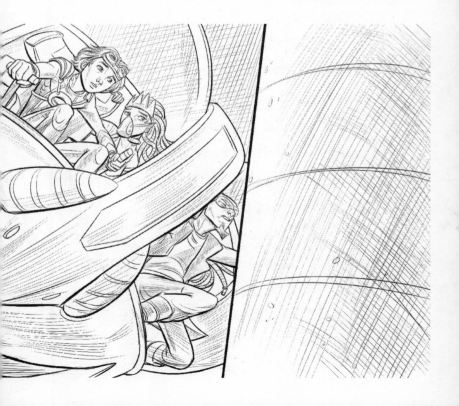

button, but the mechanism didn't respond. He raised his feet over the steering column and kicked hard against the plexiglass dome. Finally the watershield flew out and smashed on the ground.

"Come on, Lia," said Max. He wrapped an arm around the Merryn princess and helped her out of the smouldering wreckage. She clutched her spear in her webbed fingers and used it to help her stand.

"Where's Rivet?" she asked.

Max looked to where the dogbot had been clinging to the aquafly, but the wing was missing. Max felt dizzy, as though he was still bouncing along the docks. "Rivet!" he yelled. "Rivet, where are you?"

After a couple of seconds, the dogbot clambered into the building through the debris. "Max okay?" he whined. "Lia okay?"

Max's body flooded with relief. "We're

good, Rivet," he said.

"Your dogbot never asks after me," the Professor groaned as he climbed down from the craft. "Despite your landing, I'm fine!"

Max reached into the aquafly and grabbed the ray-gun. Then he led Lia, the Professor and Rivet outside through the debris. He pointed to the stacks of cargo crates lining the docks. "We can take cover behind those while we work out what to do next."

They jogged to the crates, and Max leaned against the shipping containers to catch his breath. "Siborg will be tracking us down. We need a plan to free everyone from the infection."

"What if we climb to the council chambers?" Lia said. "It has a view over the whole of Aquora. Could we shoot from there and somehow broadcast the rays over the city?"

"An obvious idea," the Professor grumbled,

"and clearly we would already be doing it, if there was any chance it would work. But there isn't enough power in the ray-gun to free the city from there."

"Wait a minute," Max said. "Couldn't we use the city's power core to amplify the tech-disrupting rays, then transmit them via the city's power lines?"

The Professor narrowed his eyes. "Perhaps... It would give it an energy boost to make the rays stronger. We could cure everyone at the same time if the frequencies are adjusted correctly."

Rivet leaped up and growled. "Someone coming, Max!"

Max heard the whine of a hover-transport followed by a clatter of boots heading in their direction. He peered out from behind the crates. A squad of fully armed defence officers were sprinting towards them. A single red eye

decorated their usually plain black uniforms.
Before Max had a chance to hide, one of
them stopped and shouted. "There they are!
Get 'em."

A volley of blaster fire exploded against the
nearest crate. Max ducked out of the way.

"We need to get out of here," he hissed to
the others. "Fast!"

CHAPTER THREE

HIGHWAY CHASE

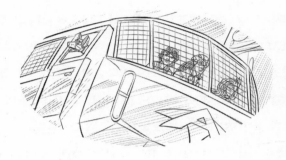

The sound of the defence officers' boots and blaster fire echoed down the narrow passages between the shipping crates. Max hurried away through the maze of stacked containers. The Professor kept at his heels along with Rivet, but Lia was falling behind. *She might be as quick as a seal underwater,* thought Max, *but on land it's a different story.*

A blaster bolt exploded close to Max as he turned a corner. The smell of melting steel filled the air. "Change of plan," he said, pulling the Professor and Lia towards the open docks.

At the end of the containers, Max spotted a robotic transport unit. It was a drab grey military version of the yellow hoverbus Max used to ride to school, except it had bars across all the windows, and armour plating. "We're going to hitch a lift," Max said.

Max ducked out into the open. Blaster fire exploded against the steel deck ahead of him. He swerved just as another blaster bolt zinged past where he had been heading. He lifted the ray-gun to return fire, but the Professor pulled a small blaster pistol from inside his coat and waved him on. "I'll hold them off," the Professor muttered as he opened fire.

Max sprinted the last few metres to the transport unit, grabbed the door release and yanked it open. Rivet raced up the steps inside, followed by Lia and the Professor. Max scrambled after them and the door closed with a hiss.

"One thing and then we can get going," Max said. He reached under the steering controls and ripped out a few wires. "There, that should switch off the autopilot. I've always wanted to drive one of these!"

Max hit the ignition button and the engines erupted into life. With a slight wobble, the hover units raised the bus off the ground. A defence officer banged the butt of his blaster against the door.

"Open in the name of Siborg," he demanded. "Or we'll blow you up!"

"Try catching us!" Max yelled. He wrenched the hoverbus into gear with a crunch and the transport unit sped away.

"Whoa!" yelled Lia as she was thrown back into her seat.

Max slammed the bus around the corner
and up the nearest ramp to the Aquoran
highway system. It was strange to see the
three lanes of the highways so empty. He
checked the rear-view mirrors. No one was
following them.

"What now?" Lia asked. She and the

Professor had strapped themselves in just behind the driver's seat.

"My dad's engineer access card will get us into the power core," Max replied. "We just need to break into my apartment and find his spare key. Then we can—"

"Max!" the Professor called. "We have company."

In the rear-view mirror, Max spotted a defence officer on a sleek chrome hoverbike. A heat haze of exhaust rippled the air behind it. The bike was the defence force's latest model. Its hover units, like two upturned wheels underneath it, could easily go faster than the transporter.

"My pistol is out of charge," the Professor said. He checked an overhead storage bin. "And I don't suppose this transport unit has weapons."

"Leave it to me," Max said. "Lia, you drive.

Keep going until you see Exit 23."

Lia wrinkled her nose. "But how do I…?"

"Just don't touch anything except the steering wheel!" Max told her, as he pushed the Professor towards the back of the bus. "We can't use a blaster on the officer," Max told him. "It's not his fault he's under Siborg's control." They stopped under an escape hatch in the roof. Max glanced through the window. The hoverbike was closing in quickly and the only weapon they had was the ray-gun.

"Professor, I have an idea," he said. "Help me up."

Max set the ray-gun on one of the seats while the Professor locked his hands together. He boosted Max to the hatch in the ceiling. The locking mechanism was stiff, but Max loosened it with a good thump. He pushed the hatch open and pulled himself out onto the roof. The force of the air streaming over the bus almost knocked him over.

"Professor," he yelled, leaning back into the bus. "Pass me the ray-gun. We should be able to stop him alerting the others."

"Since when did I become your slave?" the Professor asked, but he handed up the ray-gun anyway. Max snatched it and crouched low on the roof to stop the howling wind from blowing him off.

Max watched the defence officer race towards the hoverbus. The officer's bike engine screamed with power, and he let fly with his blaster. Bolts exploded against the edge of the roof. The bus swerved wildly across all three lanes of the highway. Max gripped the edge of the hatch. "Lia, what are you doing?" he yelled.

"Trying to stop him," Lia called back.

"Keep the bus steady – I need a clear shot,"

Max called out.

As the hoverbus straightened again, Max aimed and fired at the lone officer. The ray-gun jolted as a green beam of energy shot out, hitting the target dead on. The officer's head glowed with the tech-disrupting

energy. His hoverbike swerved, slowed, then stopped. The defence officer looked around, dazed and astonished, as the bus sped away from him. *One mindbug down, millions to go*, Max thought.

His heart lurched as he saw a dozen more hoverbikes roar onto the highway from a side ramp. The lead rider opened fire, and Max ducked, fighting to stay upright. The bus swerved and scraped along the side barriers, sending sparks up over the roof. "Watch it," Max yelled. "I'm still up here!"

"Exit 23 coming up," Lia called, as the bikes swarmed around them.

The Professor clambered onto the roof beside Max. "Give me the ray-gun," he shouted. "I have a plan."

Max crawled to the hatch and handed it over.

"Wait there!" the Professor yelled at him.

A hoverbike was closing in. Its rider had holstered his blaster and was standing on the seat of his bike, ready to leap onto the back of the bus. The Professor fired at point-blank range, hitting the officer with the ray. In confusion the defence officer tumbled from the bike and rolled across the road.

"No!" Max screamed, but the Professor just shrugged.

"Catch!" The Professor threw the ray-gun at Max. As Max caught it, his uncle rushed to the edge of the roof and leapt, landing on the empty hoverbike. He wobbled and scrambled to stay on it. *What is he doing?*

The Professor grinned from the bike and his voice crackled over Max's communicator. "Stick to the plan. I'll distract them."

The Professor performed a sharp U-turn away from the transport unit and into the oncoming hoverbikes. As he shot past the defence officers, they turned to follow him.

Max slid back inside. "I can't believe it," he said. "My uncle's actually done something brave!"

Lia shook her head. "I doubt it. He's always up to something. Hold on, we're turning off!" She swung the bus down the exit ramp at full speed. Max snatched at the back of her seat to steady himself, and Rivet barked as he slid down the bus. The hoverbus rattled off the ramp, racing along a street lined with flags showing a single red eye.

Max spotted a poster of Siborg hanging over the gleaming steel and glass entrance to his parents' apartment. "Hit the brakes, Lia," he said.

The bus jerked to a sudden halt, throwing Max and his dogbot forward again. Max reached over for the automated-driving unit controls, turned the dial to 'city tour mode' and activated it. He pulled open the door. "Quick, get off now!" he told Lia.

Max dived, hit the pavement hard and rolled with the landing. Lia and Rivet tumbled to a stop next to him. Max helped Lia to her feet as the bus rolled on down the street. "The automated-driver will confuse anyone tracking us," Max explained.

Lia shook her head. "I'm not sure it's going to matter." She pointed her spear towards the building. "It doesn't look like we can get in."

Red lasers crisscrossed the main doorway. "It'll take too long to override that," Max said. "The apartment is on full lockdown."

"Shame we can't fly," Lia said.

Max grinned at her. "No, but there are other ways to get up there!"

He crouched over his dogbot and stowed the ray-gun in Rivet's storage compartment. He strapped on his hyperblade, then opened

Rivet's control panel. He diverted power to the dogbot's magnetic paws. "We're going for a climb, Rivet," Max told him.

Rivet wagged his tail before jumping onto a narrow steel column that ran down the outside of the apartment. His paws fastened to it instantly. Max climbed onto the dogbot's back and clung on tight.

"Lia, you'll have to stand guard down here," Max said. "He can't carry both of us."

Lia looked relieved. "Be careful!"

"Come on, Rivet – up!" Max ordered.

The dogbot clanked up past floor after floor of apartments. The wind whipping around the skyscraper got stronger the higher they climbed. Max glanced down. The sight of Lia crouched with her spear way down below sent a wave of dizziness washing over him. He tightened his grip on Rivet. *Heights never used to frighten me*, thought Max. *Perhaps*

I've been underwater for too long.

At last Rivet came to a stop. "The 523rd floor, Max," he barked.

"Good boy, Rivet," Max said. "But keep quiet, we're sneaking in."

Max leaned over and stared through the window into the hallway. The picture of his mum and dad holding him as a baby had been replaced with a portrait of Siborg riding a mechanical swordfish. Max's heart hardened. Siborg was taking away everything that mattered to him. *Well, not for much longer.*

Max wedged his hyperblade under the window lock and twisted it. The window popped open without a sound. "Rivet, stay here," Max whispered, before he swung over the window ledge and slipped inside.

A delicious scent filled Max's nostrils. *I must be imagining it, he thought. That smells exactly like my mum's vegetable stew.* He shook his head and crept towards the kitchen door. The waft of spices grew stronger. He heard the clatter of plates and cutlery.

Max raised his hyperblade and quietly pushed open the kitchen door. A figure stood with her back to him, stirring a large pot of stew. Her long red hair flowed over her pale green coveralls.

"Mum?" Max breathed.

CHAPTER FOUR

FAMILY TROUBLE

Niobe spun around and put her hand to her mouth. "What are you doing here?" she hissed. "Siborg has ordered you to be killed on sight!"

"I'm here to rescue you!" Max told her.

Niobe shook her head. "It's too dangerous! Siborg has decided I'm his mother now. I cook and clean for him, and he lets me live in the apartment."

Max bit his lip. "Is Siborg here?"

"He went out this morning," Niobe said. "But he could be back any moment for his dinner." She turned back to the stew and stirred it again.

Max couldn't believe it. Had his mother given up? "I have a plan to get rid of Siborg and his mindbugs," he said. "Come with me."

"I can't. If he finds me gone, he'll know something is up," said his mother. "It'll buy you more time if I stay here."

Max hesitated. It would feel awful to leave her behind, but perhaps she was right. "Don't worry," he said. "It'll all be over soon."

"I know it will, Max," she replied. "Good luck!"

Max slipped through the doorway into the hall. The living room was the next door along. He twisted the handle carefully and eased open the door a fraction. He glimpsed the dining table and beyond it the view across the gleaming towers of Aquora, before someone shoved him from behind.

Max staggered into the living room, almost falling over.

"Glad you could join us," said the voice of Siborg.

Max's cousin sat in a high-backed black

leather chair at the other end of the room. Callum knelt beside him, staring blankly into the room. Siborg's robotic hand patted his head like a pet dog. Max felt sick seeing his father in such a powerless state. He whipped around to run out of the room, but his mum was blocking the only exit and stopped him.

She pushed me!

"Mum! What are you doing?" he demanded. "Whose side are you on?"

Niobe swept back her red hair to reveal a mindbug attached to the side of her neck. The black insect pulsed with a red light.

"You see, Max, it was just a matter of time," Siborg said. He picked up a black rectangular device with a short white antenna. "I've finally perfected a way to infect those with the Merryn Touch, like your dear mother. Or should I say, *my* dear mother? Now no one is safe from my mind control!"

"You're not getting me without a fight," Max growled. He reached for his hyperblade.

"Don't bother," Siborg said, lifting a blaster pistol from his lap. Max froze. "Now raise your hands while Mother takes away your precious hyperblade," Siborg continued. "You've been a very naughty boy."

Max clenched his fists, but raised them over his head. His mum took the blade from his belt and returned to the door.

Siborg waved the device at Max and grinned. The skin on his face puckered around his robotic implants. "You see, Max, with this I can control anyone with a mindbug implant. I can even send out a group command to make all of Aquora act as one in my name!"

Max glanced at his mum, who held the hyperblade. Siborg would shoot him before he even took a step towards it. *If only I'd*

brought the ray-gun with me, I could have evened up the odds.

"Within an hour, the mindbug infections will become permanent," said Siborg, "and the people of Aquora will be my slaves forever." He paused and sniffed the air. "Mother, is dinner ready yet?"

"Yes, my darling son," Niobe replied with a bow and then left the room, still holding Max's trusty sword.

"Mummy and Daddy will do anything for me," Siborg gloated.

Max hated to see his parents being used like playthings. "They'll never be your true parents," he snapped, and took a step closer. "You can't treat them like slaves."

"Can't I?" Max froze as Siborg pressed the pistol against Callum's temple. But there was nothing he could do about it. Siborg sneered. "You're sentimental, that's your problem.

That's why you'll never beat me."

The vid-screen in the corner of the room flickered into life. "Incoming call," it announced before the tall, thin figure of Lieutenant Jared appeared on the screen.

Jared's piercing blue eyes gazed at Siborg. "Your lordship, my men have captured the Professor," he said. "I wouldn't have disturbed you, but he insisted that we contact you with an offer of an alliance!"

Max tried to control his breathing. He couldn't believe it! After all they had been through to defeat the mindbugs and Siborg, the Professor had finally betrayed them. *I should have been expecting it*, Max realised. *But we were so close to defeating Siborg.*

Siborg snorted. "The Professor isn't fit to polish my battle suit. Execute him."

Max swallowed. Whatever the Professor had done, he didn't deserve that!

"No, wait…" Siborg said. "Why deprive me of the pleasure of doing it myself? Jared, keep him locked up until I get to you. There's no need to make him comfortable."

"Yes, sir." Jared saluted smartly before vanishing from the vid-screen.

Max eyed Siborg nervously, and an icy cold shiver ran down his spine. *What does he have planned for me?* Max wondered. *Mindbug infection…or death?*

"I hope my dinner doesn't get cold while I'm away," said Siborg, standing up. "Killing always works up my appetite." His robotic red eye and brown human eye stared at Max, as he holstered the blaster pistol and headed for the door.

"Don't think you can get away with this," Max said.

As Siborg opened the living room door, he paused. "I never thought about having a brother," he said. "But, you know, I do so enjoy being an only child." Siborg pressed some buttons on the remote control and pointed it at Max's dad. "I know we're family, but keeping you alive is too much of a risk, Max." He pressed another button. "Father, dispose of him!"

Max gasped as the door locked behind Siborg. Callum slowly got to his feet. His eyes narrowed with the cool glint of a killer, then he crackled his knuckles and took a step towards Max.

CHAPTER FIVE

JOURNEY UNDER AQUORA

"Dad, it's me, Max, you've got to remember," Max pleaded. "You need to fight Siborg's control before it's too late!"

Max edged behind his mother's collection of ancient Merryn coral masks. Callum sprang forward and kicked aside a table. The fragile masks shattered against the floor. Pale pink and yellow coral fragments crunched under Callum's boots.

"Dad, you don't have to do what he wants!"

Max glanced around for something to defend himself with. At the other end of the table was a large platinum bowl decorated with gold, given to his dad for long service to Aquora. *Maybe I can knock Dad out with it...* Callum lunged at him and Max dived. He crawled under the table, fighting through the chair legs. "Rivet!" Max yelled, hoping the dogbot could hear him.

Max scrambled out from under the table and grabbed the metal dish. Callum landed on his back. Max crashed into the carpet and the dish went spinning across the room. His dad's weight held him down. Callum's large hands wrapped around his neck and squeezed.

Max couldn't breathe. Blood pounded in his head as he gasped for air. "No, Dad," he wheezed as the fingers gripped tighter. "You don't want this. Siborg wants this."

Max's vision dimmed. His eyes felt like they were going to pop from his skull. *This is it*, Max thought. *I've failed....*

Something crashed through the living room window and Callum was knocked off him. Max rolled over, gasping for air. Rivet and Callum were tumbling across the carpet. *Good boy*, Max thought.

Rivet pinned Callum's arms down with his powerful front paws. "Bad dad," Rivet barked.

Time to put an end to this, Max thought. He staggered over and removed the ray-gun from the dogbot's storage compartment. He aimed at his father's head and pulled the trigger. A beam of intense green light blasted Callum's face and a ghostly glow surrounded him.

Max watched his dad shake and tremble on the floor. His face twisted in pain as the mindbug infection was destroyed. Callum turned toward Max. His eyes had lost the hard edge that Siborg's control had given them.

"I'm so sorry, Max," he said. "I…I…"

Max took a deep breath. "It's all right, Dad," he said. "It wasn't you, it was Siborg. Rivet, get off him."

The dogbot climbed off Callum's front. As Callum stood, he reached for the mindbug on his lower spine and ripped it off. He threw it out of the window.

"I need your help to stop Siborg before the rest of Aquora's infection becomes permanent," Max said.

"Over my dead body!" Max's mother gasped from the doorway.

Max spun around. Niobe held a tray with a bowl of steaming stew and a freshly baked bread roll. As Max brought the gun to bear, she flung the entire tray towards him.

Max ducked and fired at the same time. The bowl sailed through the broken apartment window and Niobe dropped to the floor. Her hands and arms twitched as spasms rocked her body. Max raced to her side and held her until the shaking stopped. She opened her eyes and looked up at him. "Max," she said softly. "Is that really you?"

"You're free of Siborg's control now," he said.

Niobe smiled and reached under her hair. With a wince, she ripped the mindbug from her neck and threw it aside. Rivet caught it and crushed it with his jaws.

"Max?" Niobe asked frowning. "What are we going to do about the rest of Aquora?"

Max helped his mum to stand up. "That's why I'm here," he said. He turned to Callum. "Dad, where is your engineering access card?"

"It's in the safe." Callum crossed the room and removed a portrait of Siborg riding Fliktor the Deadly Conqueror from the wall to reveal a high-tech safe. He pressed his hand against the scanner and spoke his name. The safe swung open and Callum pulled out the keycard along with a couple of small blasters.

He strapped one onto his thigh and threw the other to Niobe. "Let's save Aquora!"

"We need to find a way to spread this tech-disrupting beam across the whole city," Max said, showing the ray-gun to his dad.

Callum examined the weapon and shook his head. "It's impossible," he said, passing the ray-gun to Niobe. "It doesn't have the power supply needed to create a beam powerful enough."

"The ray-gun uses a crystal to generate the right frequency," Max explained. "We just need to amplify that signal."

"Your father's right," Niobe began, then stopped. "No, wait! What if we used the city's energy grid?"

"We'd have to fire it into the source of Aquora's electricity – the power core," Callum said. "It's a giant ball of plasma protected underneath the entire city."

"The sooner we get there," Max said, "the sooner we can stop Siborg!"

"Here," Niobe said, handing back his hyperblade. "You'll need this."

Max gripped the sword and led his parents down the hallway to the front door. He peered down the corridor leading to the lifts. It was empty. He sprinted to the controls and hit the down button. One of the lifts opened instantly. Max jerked his hyperblade forward, expecting an attack.

Callum put his hand on his shoulder. "Siborg reprogrammed the lifts so he never had to wait!"

Max, his parents and Rivet jumped inside and pressed for the lobby. *We could be going out as a family for a walk*, he thought, *except we have a city to save!*

Max watched the floor numbers drop on the lift's display. Callum paced the small elevator, muttering to himself. Niobe held Max tightly and smoothed his hair with her hand.

At last, "Lobby" appeared on the floor display. Max moved to the front as the elevator doors opened. Max's communicator unit buzzed into life.

"Max, quick!" Lia said. "Lots of defence officers are coming!"

Max rushed across the foyer with his parents and Rivet. Through the glass doors of the building, he spotted a squad of Aquoran defence officers closing on their position. Lia crouched outside behind potted shrubs clipped into the shape of Siborg. She gripped her spear, but it wouldn't be much use against the blasters.

The apartments' entrance was still blocked by a crisscross of lasers. "Dad, can you switch off the lockdown?" Max asked.

Callum swiped his keycard over the security controls and tapped in a number. The lasers vanished and Max scrambled out to Lia. "Are you okay?"

Lia bit her lip and nodded. Max's parents dived beside them. A blaster bolt exploded in the shrubs above. Max brushed the burnt leaves off his deepsuit. "Dad, what's the fastest way to the power core from here?"

Callum pointed to the corner of the building. "There's an engineering access shaft in that alleyway," he said.

Max peered over the top of the pots. Defence officers were pushing forward. He fired the ray-gun at the nearest one. He couldn't waste time curing them all, but freeing a couple from Siborg's control might slow them down. He fired at another before ducking away.

"Let's go, Dad!" Max said.

Exploding blaster bolts chased them as they raced along the building. Shattered glass rained down on the pavement and crunched underfoot. Niobe stumbled, but Max caught her before she fell over. He ushered her around the corner as he pinned down a couple of defence officers with blasts from the ray-gun.

"Quick, Max!" Callum called. He stood at the bottom of some concrete steps in a narrow alleyway. Max and Niobe charged after him.

"In here," Callum said, swiping his card outside a steel door in the next building. He pulled open the door. Max, Lia, Rivet and Niobe ducked into a short concrete service tunnel. Callum slammed the door behind him. Dim lights came on.

"Just need to make some adjustments to the controls before we can open the next door," Callum said, pushing past Max to the far end of the tunnel.

Max removed a small light from his deepsuit and held it up so his dad could see what he was doing. Sweat was dripping down Callum's forehead as he pulled the panel from the door and rewired the controls.

Fists thundered against the steel door from the alleyway. The defence officers had found them! "Dad, we're running out of time!" Max warned.

"Almost ready," Callum muttered as he twisted a couple of wires together. "There!"

The door to the engineering sector hissed open. Blaster bolts exploded against the thick metal door to the street.

Max, Callum, Niobe, Rivet and Lia rushed

through the open door onto a metal-mesh platform. It hung from thick cables in what looked like an elevator shaft. More mesh formed a wall with a handrail around the platform, but the elevator had no ceiling. A row of deepsuits hung along one wall.

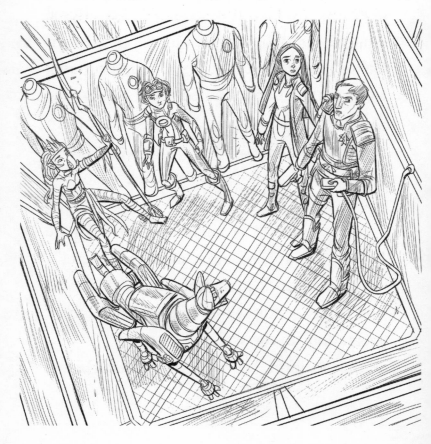

Callum closed the door behind Max and then fired his blaster at the controls, which sparked and fizzed.

"That should delay them," he said, before picking up a yellow control box connected to a thick rubber-coated cable. The whole platform shuddered as winches above them groaned into life.

The elevator sank down the shaft into the darkness below. "Next stop, the city's power core," Callum said.

I just hope we're in time, Max thought.

CHAPTER SIX

AMBUSH

Max gripped the ray-gun tightly and wondered how long it would take to reach the power core. Lia nervously eyed the cables lowering the rattling metal platform down the shaft into the gloom. The cables squealed as though they could snap at any moment.

Flashing amber lights and sirens erupted around the platform. Rivet scrambled to his feet and barked.

"It's okay," Callum said. "Don't worry,

Rivet. It's just routine."

He crossed to the row of deepsuits pegged to the side of the lift. Max frowned as Callum slipped one over his uniform and handed another deepsuit to Niobe.

"Are we going underwater?" Max asked.

Niobe nodded as she zipped up the deepsuit. "Aquora's main power core is on the seabed and surrounded by water to control its temperature."

Callum rummaged in a locker and pulled out an Amphibio mask. "We're about halfway down," he said, before strapping it on. "Everyone needs to grab hold of the handrail before we hit the water," he ordered through the mask. "We can't slow the platform if you are washed away. Keep a tight hold."

Max tucked the ray-gun into his deepsuit and Lia wedged her spear into the floor before they grabbed hold of the rail. "What about Rivet?" she asked.

Max glanced at his dogbot. "Rivet, magnetise paws."

Rivet's paws clunked against the wire mesh. Through the holes in the floor, Max caught the reflection of the flashing amber lights in the water they were plunging towards.

The platform shook as it smacked into the surface. Water rushed up through the gaps in the floor. Max could taste the taint of grease and oil through his gills, as the platform sank into darkness. Max pulled out the ray-gun and turned a dial on its side. The crystal inside begin to whine. Lia took a step back and Callum's eyes were questioning behind his dive mask.

"Set to maximum power," said Niobe.

Max nodded. The crystal inside began to glow brighter, as the ray-gun charged. *I just hope this works*, Max thought. He knew that with the ray-gun set at such a high energy output it was likely the crystal would burn out when fired. *I've got one shot.*

Max spied a glowing red light ahead and the platform slowed before clanking to a halt beside an open horizontal shaft. He swam forward into an enormous chamber shaped like a giant hollow ball. The water was as warm as the seas off a tropical island.

A chequerboard of solid plates and gaps covered the walls. Through the gaps another layer of plates and holes could be seen. "There are seven layers in all," Callum said through the deepsuit's in-built communicator as he passed Max. "It protects the power core and lets the ocean cool it naturally."

Max swam closer to the pulsing ball of energy that dominated the centre of the chamber. Blue-and-silver plasma swirled over its surface. Light pulsed through it in waves, making the thick cables that snaked from it glow with energy. The largest cables slithered towards the lift shaft and up towards the city. Max noticed that several cables seemed to be going out into the sea.

"Dad, where do those cables go?" he asked.

Callum stood on a small platform halfway up the other side of the chamber. Behind him were rows of blinking lights and control panels. He peered down at Max. "Those go to the seabed," he said. "The power core is ancient tech from the earliest days of Aquora. It's designed to take geothermal energy drawn from deep inside Nemos and convert it into electricity. The other cables supply energy to the entire city. I need to adjust the power grid settings otherwise the ray-gun will set off an automated shutdown."

Max swam closer to the giant ball of plasma. Heat radiated through the water into his deepsuit. His skin tingled with excitement. He'd never seen so much energy stored in one place. It was strange to think the city would be helpless without this power source.

"Danger, Max!" Rivet growled. His ears twisted towards the lift shaft. With a clank, a series of skeletal legs landed inside the lift platform.

"Cyrates!" Max yelled. He reached for his hyperblade. The ray-gun, he noticed, had reached full charge. Over a dozen cyrates rushed forward, their weapons pointed towards the plasma ball. Niobe readied her blaster and Lia gripped her spear.

Siborg's voice boomed from a speaker on the nearest cyrate. "Fighting in here would be a mistake. If one stray shot hits the power core, you can say goodbye to Aquora forever!"

The cyrates all drew gleaming hyperblade cutlasses in perfect unison.

Max saw his mum lower her blaster. "He's right," she said grimly.

Max holstered his own ray-gun, and unsheathed his hyperblade. *We'll have to do this the old-fashioned way*. He eyed the cyrates nervously; none of them had seen Callum up on the control platform making adjustments. The plan could still work.

But Siborg's robotic minions didn't attack. Instead, they turned towards the lift shaft. Max gasped as a massive robot landed inside the lift with a thud. Large red spikes stuck out from its head above two glowing yellow eyes. Hatches opened along the robot's silver arms and legs to reveal a range of missiles and blasters with laser sights.

The hatches closed again. A large black panel on the robot's chest turned transparent and Siborg stared out at Max. He narrowed his one human eye.

"Do you like my new battle suit?" he said with a sneer.

Siborg raised one of the suit's long silver arms. The Professor dangled by his collar from a red robotic claw.

"My pathetic father has informed me of

your little plan." Siborg's voice boomed from the speakers.

"You!" Lia yelled. "Betrayer! You were

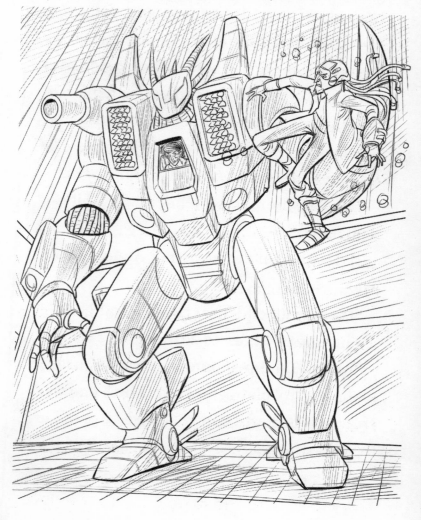

supposed to distract Siborg, not make a deal with him!"

"It's clear that negotiations are still ongoing," the Professor snapped. He squirmed under the claw. "Besides, when we arrived in Siborgia, it made sense to side with a winning team. Siborg is my son after all, so it's no surprise he would be victorious."

I shouldn't be surprised, thought Max. *The Professor's always looked out for himself first.*

"Now it's time to surrender, Max," Siborg demanded.

"I'd rather die than betray Aquora," said Max.

Siborg grinned. "That can be arranged."

The cyrates began to advance.

"Max!" Callum shouted. Everyone turned to the control platform above. Max's dad was crouched behind a control panel. "I've made the adjustments!"

It might be too late for us, but there's still a chance for Aquora! Max realised. He spun around and fired the green beam of the tech-disrupting ray into the power core.

CHAPTER SEVEN

SIBORG'S REVENGE

"No!" Siborg screamed.

Max kept firing at the power core. It hummed with the tech-disrupting beam's frequency. The blue-and-silver plasma changed colour and threw a green glow over the chamber.

Green light pulsed into the cables stretching from the power core into the city. The beam spluttered and died. *The circuits must have overheated*, Max realised. *I hope it lasted long enough to save the city!*

Max turned to his cousin and threw the useless ray-gun at him. It bounced off the clear viewing screen in the battle suit's chest. "Here, keep it," Max said.

Siborg shook the suit's fist at him. "What have you done?" he bellowed. "Cyrates, attack!"

The soldier droids surged forwards. Some raised cutlasses as others charged up their blaster rifles. Max dived at the nearest cyrate. He sliced off its arm then smashed its face with the blade hilt. It collapsed to the floor.

Max stepped towards the next cyrate, but before he reached it Lia had skewered it through the chest with her spear. His mum surged past and blasted two cyrates at point-blank range.

"Behind you, Max!" Callum shouted from the control platform.

Max spun around. Two cyrates were rushing towards him. A blaster bolt from Max's dad exploded into one cyrate's chest. As it toppled backwards, Max jumped over its body and sliced the head off the other cyrate.

"Thanks, Dad!" Max called back.

"Give it back!" A scream from Lia sent Max scrambling towards her. She was wresting her spear back from a cyrate.

"Rivet," Max yelled. "Help Lia!"

The dogbot swam over and snapped at the cyrate's leg, taking it off with his metal jaws. Lia twisted the spear and sent the cyrate flying back towards Siborg.

"Here, Max!" Niobe threw Max a cyrate's blaster. "Let's finish this for good."

As the last cyrate collapsed, Max turned to Siborg. The giant battle suit had retreated to the lift platform with the Professor still dangling from a claw.

"Surrender!" Max yelled. "It's over!"

Siborg grinned from inside the viewing panel on the front of the suit. "Never," he said.

"Siborg," Niobe said. "Give yourself up. You can still lead a normal life. We can help you once you've served your time for your crimes."

"You think this is over?" Siborg laughed. "I always have a back-up plan!"

The entire chamber shook as if there was a seaquake. The light from the core flickered. The wrenching and grinding sound of metal being torn apart reverberated from outside and around the chamber. Small fragments of metal fell through the gaps in the protective layers. Max swam back as the inside layer buckled and twisted. He gripped his hyperblade and blaster. He had a nasty feeling he knew what Siborg had summoned.

The head of Gulak, the gulper eel, smashed

through the last layer. It spat out broken panels and metal supports. The hole wasn't quite big enough for it to get into the chamber. It widened its massive jaws and crushed the surrounding walls until they crumpled out of its way. The arrow-shaped head of

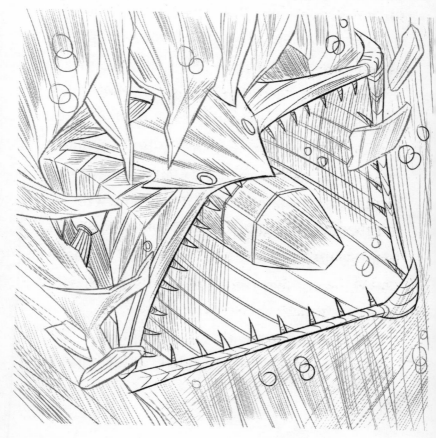

the Robobeast broke fully into the chamber, peering around with its close-set eyes.

Siborg laughed from inside his battle suit. "You see! Gulak's jaws can bite through anything," he said. "I gave it orders to burrow through the walls surrounding this chamber. Once I activate my Robobeast's self-destruct, the power of the explosion will set off the power core and destroy the whole of Aquora!"

"You can't do that," Max gasped. "It's madness!"

"No, it's revenge, cousin," Siborg replied. "You might have ruined my plans for Siborgia, but if I can't rule over the city, no one will!"

The Professor tried to pull himself free of Siborg's claws. "How am I supposed to make the Aquorans fear me – I mean, us – if they're all dead?"

"You're joining them," Siborg replied.

The Professor's face paled, then Siborg

dropped him. He landed on top of a broken cyrate with a bump.

"We could still be partners," the Professor pleaded. "Think of what we could achieve together! We could fashion a new world in our image. I don't want to die!"

"Shut up!" Siborg snapped. "You had your chance years ago before you abandoned me. You're nothing but a worthless, treacherous worm." Siborg's arm shot up and pointed at him. "Gulak, get rid of this nuisance!"

The thrusters dotted along Gulak's body fired into action. The gaping mouth of the Robobeast surged across the chamber towards Max's uncle.

"No!" the Professor cried. His feet slipped as he tried to scramble over the cyrate bodies.

I have to stop Gulak, Max realised. *Once he eats the Professor, he'll destroy Aquora!* Max kicked through the water and swung his

hyperblade against the Robobeast's neck.
The blade rang against the toughened metal
without even making a dent.

"I'm too young and brilliant to die!" Max's

uncle cried before the eel's mouth closed over him.

With a gulp, the Professor was gone.

CHAPTER EIGHT

THE FINAL COUNTDOWN

Niobe screamed. "No!"

Max thrust his hyperblade between Gulak's locked teeth. He yanked the blade back and forth to prise them apart. The Robobeast shook its blunt arrow-shaped head and sent Max flying across the chamber.

Max crashed into the wall. The air exploded from his lungs. His body throbbed with pain, but he clutched the hyperblade ready to fight. Instead of coming after him, Gulak's thrusters

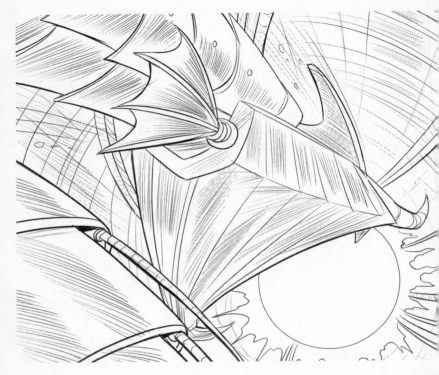

powered the eel towards Aquora's energy core.

The Robobeast snaked its long body around the silver-and-blue matrix before clamping its jaws tightly to the pulsing core.

"Gulak, activate self-destruct sequence," Siborg boomed.

Red lights flashed along the robotic creature's jaws then down its spine to its tail. "Self-destruct activated. Five minutes remaining," a computerised voice announced from the Robobeast's speakers.

Siborg raised his robotic arms. Rocket flames shot out from under his boots. The battle suit lifted up from the chamber floor towards the hole in the protective sphere. "Enjoy the fireworks!"

"Siborg, you're under arrest," Callum shouted from the platform. "Surrender, or I will open fire."

Siborg gave a strangely hollow metallic laugh that echoed around the tunnel. Callum fired his blaster at Siborg, but the bolts ricocheted off the armour.

Max couldn't believe his cousin was crazy enough to kill everyone. He launched himself after Siborg, swimming as fast as could. Siborg's battle suit might be blaster-proof but Max could still stop him from escaping. *Siborg will have to stop the countdown if his own life is in peril,* Max thought.

Max followed Siborg into the tunnel ripped into the protective layers of the chamber. Siborg had stopped close to the other end. A dozen figures on swordfish had appeared out of the gloom ahead, led by King Salinus.

Max had never been gladder to see the Merryn ruler and his warriors.

"You're cornered, Siborg," he shouted. "Surrender."

Siborg's long battle-suit arm reached for something strapped to his back – a dark grey cube. Its edges glowed red like lava.

A sea grenade! Max panicked. *I've got to stop him!* He hurled his hyperblade at Siborg. The blade sliced through the water and pierced the battle suit's shoulder. Black fluid oozed from the hydraulic power systems. Siborg cried out in frustration as his whole suit stopped moving.

A chill ran down the back of Max's deepsuit. "Watch out!" he yelled to the Merryn. "It's going to explode!"

The grenade, still clutched in Siborg's grip, burst into white light. The suit went spinning one way, its blackened and twisted arm the other. Max stared as it swept past. The suit sank towards the power core, with Siborg battering his fists against the viewing screen.

"Warning!" the voice boomed from Gulak's head. "One minute to detonation! Warning! One minute to detonation!"

Plasma erupted from under the battle suit as it crashed into the power core. Siborg's eyes widened as sparks leapt from the controls around him. He twisted around wildly. A pale yellow vapour was filling his compartment. Unexpectedly, the viewing screen blinked and turned black. Max stared, stunned. Could Siborg survive in there?

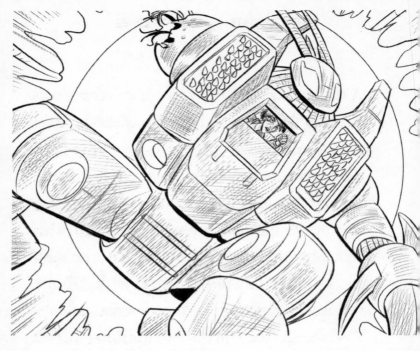

"Max!" Niobe yelled. "We need to get Gulak away from the power core."

"Dad, help me release its jaws!" Max called, retrieving his hyperblade quickly from the tunnel in the metal mesh.

Max and Callum dived to the Robobeast's head. Gulak's jaws were stretched wide to take hold of the power core's sphere. Max spied a gap big enough for him to crawl inside where the jaws were hinged.

Callum handed Max a torch from his deepsuit. His hands shook as he angled the beam into Gulak's mouth. The light glinted over the gulper eel's curved teeth. Max swallowed and wriggled inside. The back of the eel's mouth was sealed off with thick metal shutters. *The Professor's in there somewhere*, Max realised.

He searched for the controls of the Robobeast's jaws. The light glinted off a metallic box. *The control circuits!* It was locked. Max swung his hyperblade at it, but a sharp pain jarred up his arm and the sword rebounded off the metal.

"Forty-five…forty-four…forty-three…" the mechanical voice counted down.

Max swept his hand across the sides of the Robobeast's mouth, looking for where the hydraulic-fluid pipes might be located. He found a section of mouth with thick vein-like structures just under the surface and jammed his hyperblade into them.

As Max pulled the sword out, a black stream of hydraulic fluid squirted from the Robobeast. With a loud hiss that made Max's heart leap, the jaws opened. Max dived out. "Gulak's free of the power core!" he yelled.

"Thirty seconds remaining," Gulak's self-destruct computer announced.

"Help the others!" Callum yelled as he

waved Max towards a rope tied to the Robobeast's tail. King Salinus and his warriors were already heaving Gulak towards the hole in the protective sphere.

"Max, over here!" Lia called from where she and Niobe were pulling on ropes. Max and his dad slipped alongside Lia and grasped the ropes. *We're going to need all the help we can get*, Max thought.

"Rivet," he yelled. "Tug on this rope."

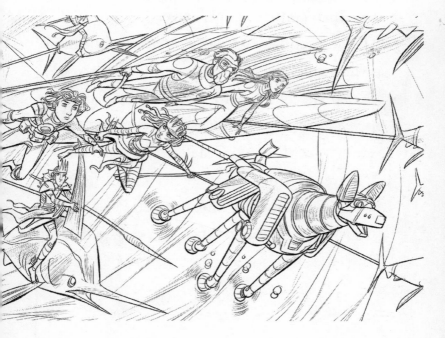

The dogbot clamped down on the end of the rope and started pulling. They swam into the tunnel, dragging Gulak behind them.

"Ten seconds to detonation," the speakers announced. "Nine…"

"Faster!" Niobe said. "It's not far enough away to stop it damaging the power core!"

Max could feel the gills on his neck strain with effort. As the Merryn pulling the ropes had reached the end of the tunnel, their swordfish came to help heave.

"Five seconds," Gulak's speakers boomed as the gulper eel slid into open water.

With the extra help of the swordfish, the power core was getting smaller and smaller as everyone dragged Gulak into the ocean.

"Three seconds…" the voice announced.

"Get away now!" Callum yelled.

A Merryn grabbed Max and dragged him from the Robobeast. His parents and Lia were being carried by other warriors as Gulak started sinking.

"Detonating," the voice announced.

Gulak lit up the ocean with a blazing ball of fire, quickly extinguished by the water. The shockwave sent Max tumbling through the water, not knowing which way was up or down. The force of the explosion left grey blots in his eyes, temporarily blinding him.

Max heard the dogbot's propellers first, then saw Rivet's silhouette in the water. His sight was improving. Max could make out the debris from the gulper eel floating down towards the bottom of the sea. He gripped Rivet's collar, staring after it.

The Professor's dead, Max realised in horror. *No one could have survived that.*

CHAPTER NINE

A DIFFERENT LIFE

"Find Mum and Dad, Rivet," Max said.

Rivet dragged him towards the seabed. Pieces of Gulak were scattered across the sandy floor. Max spotted two figures searching through the wreckage with a Merryn guard.

"Dad! Mum!" Max shouted as he recognised his parents. They waved and swam up to him.

"Max, thank Nemos you're okay," Niobe

said. Despite the smile, Niobe looked as though she were trying hard not to cry. "My brother's gone for good," she added, softly.

Max took her hand. His chest ached for his uncle, even though he had betrayed their plans to Siborg. Max scanned the seabed

around them. He hoped to spot even a shred of the Professor's lab coat. Twisted metal scales and broken spikes from the gulper eel's fins nestled among the scrawny sea-scrub that grew beneath the city.

Max squeezed his mum's hand. "He didn't die in vain. If Aquora is free of the mindbugs, it'll be thanks to the Professor's ray-gun."

She blinked back her tears and nodded. "We should check what's going on up there," she said.

Max kicked out and together they swam back towards the surface. Callum and Rivet were close behind but King Salinus and his hunting party were heading off in another direction. Lia shot away from them on Spike towards Max. "My father hopes the Breathers are free from Siborg's cursed machines," she said over the communicator.

The sunlight got brighter. Max and his

family burst into the fresh air. At once a loud cheer erupted around them. Max blinked and gazed up at the docks. Aquorans lined every available viewing space. They pressed up against the railings. Children sat on their parents' shoulders. Everyone waved at Max and his parents.

"You freed us! You saved Aquora from the mindbugs!" they shouted.

"We did it!" Max punched the air. "Our plan worked!"

Then Max spotted Jared with a group of defence officers. The pride on his stern face seemed mixed with a hint of embarrassment. He pointed towards a small rescue craft and ordered his men into it.

When the defence officers' boat reached them, they pulled Max out of the water first, followed by his mum and finally his dad. Max hugged his parents through the foil blankets the rescuers had given them. They had defeated Siborg and his plan to take over Aquora. But even better, he had both his parents back.

***

Max stood in the observation room overlooking Aquora's most advanced and secure lab. Defence officers guarded laboratory doorways. Max pressed his face against the glass window and stared down at the giant battle suit secured in the middle of the room.

Technicians in white lab-coats rushed between medical scanners and sensors brought in from the engineering department. The front panel of Siborg's battle suit had been prised open. Apparently, Max's half-human and half-machine cousin had been fused into the suit by his encounter with the power core, and after twenty-seven hours of

delicate operations they weren't sure they could get him out alive. The Chief Medic overseeing the work spoke to one of the technicians before rushing out of the lab door.

Max glanced at his father, who had an arm wrapped around Niobe. Callum had insisted Aquora did what it could to save Siborg's life, so he could face justice. Max wasn't sure what he wanted. If his cousin did wake up, he'd never be happy until he escaped and built more Robobeasts to enslave the entire planet.

The observation room door slide open. The Chief Medic stepped in, holding a tablet in his hands. He had dark circles under his eyes from supervising the already lengthy operation.

"We think we can extract him from the suit safely," he said.

"Will he be all right?" Niobe asked.

"We don't know," the Chief Medic replied, staring at his notes. "We've never worked on a patient with cybernetic modifications before."

Niobe wiped her eyes and sniffed. "I know he's done terrible things, but he's all I have left of my brother. We couldn't even find a trace of the Professor's body to bury."

Max looked down again at his cousin's mangled form. Life could have been different for Siborg. What if he hadn't been neglected by the Professor? He might not have grown up so bitter and resentful. But was it too late now? Perhaps with Niobe and Callum caring for him, Siborg could change for the better.

Max gazed at his parents. He felt luckier than ever to have such kind and loving parents. They always did what they thought was best, even if it was a difficult decision. He could feel a lump forming in his throat and turned to look at Lia.

The Merryn princess sat in the corner with an Amphibio mask on, keeping Rivet entertained. She dangled a carved coral fish on a piece of seaweed and was encouraging him try to catch it. Rivet tilted his head with a puzzled look and gave her a rather unimpressed stare.

Max laughed. Lia looked up and smiled at him. *I'm lucky to have brave and loyal friends too*, he thought. *Ones who've stuck with me on all our Quests.*

He glanced down again at Siborg and his charred battle suit. One thing was certain. Whether Siborg survived or not, there would be other dangers lurking in the seas of Nemos. *But as long as I've got my family and friends to support me*, Max thought, *I'll be ready for them.*

Don't miss Max's next Sea Quest adventure,
when he faces

VELOTH
THE VAMPIRE SQUID

Look out for all the books in
Sea Quest Series 7:

THE LOST STARSHIP

VELOTH THE VAMPIRE SQUID
GLENDOR THE STEALTHY SHADOW
MIRROC THE GOBLIN SHARK
BLISTRA THE SEA DRAGON

OUT IN MARCH 2016!

Don't miss the
BRAND NEW
Special Bumper Edition:

JANDOR
THE ARCTIC LIZARD

OUT IN NOVEMBER 2015

WIN AN EXCLUSIVE
GOODY BAG

In every Sea Quest book the Sea Quest logo is
hidden in one of the pictures. Find the logos in books
21-24, make a note of which pages they appear on and
go online to enter the competition at

www.seaquestbooks.co.uk

Each month we will put all of the correct entries into a draw
and select one winner to receive a special Sea Quest goody bag.

You can also send your entry on a postcard to:

Sea Quest Competition, Orchard Books,
Carmelite House, 50 Victoria Embankment,
London, EC4Y 0DZ

Don't forget to include your name and address!

GOOD LUCK

Closing Date: Dec 30th 2015

IF YOU LIKE SEA QUEST, YOU'LL LOVE BEAST QUEST!

Series 1: COLLECT THEM ALL!

An evil wizard has enchanted the magical beasts of Avantia. Only a true hero can free the beasts and save the land. Is Tom the hero Avantia has been waiting for?

978 1 84616 483 5

978 1 84616 482 8

978 1 84616 484 2

978 1 84616 486 6

978 1 84616 485 9

978 1 84616 487 3

DON'T MISS THE
BRAND NEW SERIES OF:

Series 15: VELMAL'S REVENGE

978 1 40833 487 4

978 1 40833 489 8

978 1 40833 491 1

978 1 40833 493 5

COMING SOON